Licensed exclusively to Top That Publishing Ltd
Tide Mill Way, Woodbridge, Suffolk, IP12 1AP, UK
www.topthatpublishing.com
Copyright © 2013 Tide Mill Media
All rights reserved
2 4 6 8 9 7 5 3 1
Manufactured in China

Written by Oakley Graham
Illustrated by Dan Crisp

ISBN 978-1-78244-352-0

A catalogue record for this book is available from the British Library

The Magic Balloon

Written by Oakley Graham

Illustrated by Dan Crisp

Many, many years ago, in the city of Montreal,
Lived a boy called Will, who was very, very tall.
Will was a great inventor and was over the moon,
When he created the world's first magic balloon.

The basket was woven from smelly odd socks,
And sandbags were fashioned from second-hand frocks.
The balloon was a mixture of textures and colours,
Made from old woollen tights and pants from his brothers.

Will travelled in his bright balloon across the USA,
It twinkled in the open sky as he made his way.

From the Empire State to the Golden Gate, and everything in between,
His multicoloured, magic balloon handled like a dream.

As the cold wind blew, Will travelled south for a vacation,
He landed in the treetops of the amazing Amazon basin.
From this makeshift hide, young Will spied animals of every colour,
A jaguar and a spectacled bear that reminded him of his mother.

Flying at a steady pace, the balloon crossed the Atlantic,
From the basket, Will did spot, some whales that were gigantic.

The coast of Africa came
into view far off on the horizon.
Lions and elephants roamed the
plains and some friendly tribesmen.

So much to do, so much to see,
where did Will travel next?
He really didn't know where to go,
so he sent his dad a text.
'Go to Europe, Asia and the Middle East,'
that was his dad's advice.
'Paris, Delhi, Kathmandu,
and visit London twice.'

Will took his dad's advice (he didn't want to be a failure),
And after travelling for seven months he set off for Australia.
Uluru and angry kangaroos were part of his adventure,
But Will was feeling lonely and so homewards he did venture.

Many, many years ago, in the city of Montreal,
Lived a boy called Will, who was very, very tall.
He travelled around the world and was over the moon,
When he returned back home in his magic balloon.